For Charlie and Oscar, and their granddaddies

First edition 2007

Library of Congress Cataloging-in-Publication Data is available.

Library of Congress Catalog Card Number 2006040086

ISBN 978-0-7636-3089-8

2 4 6 8 10 9 7 5 3 1

Printed in Singapore

This book was typeset in Cafeteria.
The illustrations were created digitally.

Candlewick Press
2067 Massachusetts Avenue
Cambridge, Massachusetts 02140

visit us at www.candlewick.com

One day, Sock Monkey, the famous toy actor, received a very important telephone call.

Hello?

You're WANTED FOR THE PART OF "RED REARDON" IN OUR SINGING COWBOY MOVIE, "HUBBUB AT THE HAPPY CANYON HOEDOWN!"

Sock Monkey had to get busy and prepare. He called his friends and asked them to help.

To show Sock Monkey how to yodel, Miss Bunn took him on a crazy airplane ride. She played cowboy music while flying loop-de-loops.

Next, Froggie gave Sock Monkey a horseback riding lesson.
Froggie's horse, Stardust, was thrilled to be helping such a
famous actor.

Git along, li'l piggie.

And Blue Pig dressed like a cow, then ran around and around until Sock Monkey got good enough with the lasso to catch him.

Sock Buddy lent Sock Monkey one of his many sensational cowboy outfits, then helped him get all decked out.

Sock Monkey was ready to begin making his movie. Almost . . .

Then he met Lulu Nevada, the actress he was supposed to kiss!

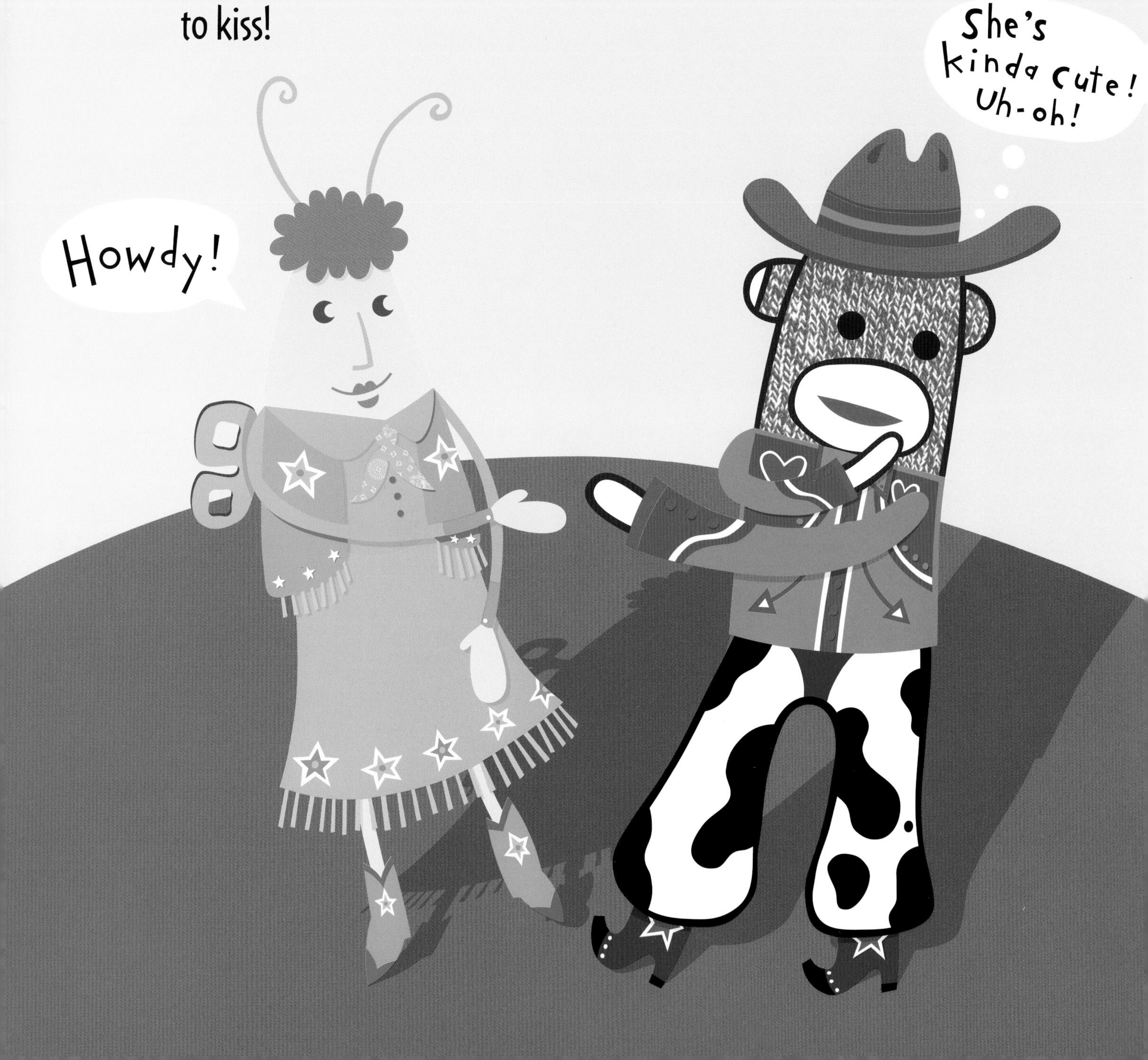

Sock Monkey tried to talk to the director about the big kiss,
but . . .

the filming had begun!

Sock Monkey aced all his scenes.
He yodeled melodiously and rode his horse handsomely
and lassoed the cow skillfully. Everything was going great!

LUNCH BREAK!
NEXT SCENE: THE
BIG KISS!

Sock Monkey wobbled in his boots as he walked over to his trailer. His friends had prepared a delicious lunch for him. But Sock Monkey couldn't eat.

Oooohh

Finally, it was time to film the big KISS!

Sock Monkey and Lulu began to sing . . .

and inch closer and closer together.

Lulu leaned in toward Sock Monkey . . .

Sock Monkey shuffled over to Lulu and apologized.

But no matter what he said, Lulu wept and wept.

Sock Monkey felt terrible. He realized there was only one thing he could do. . . .

Sock Monkey kissed Lulu!
Right on the cheek!

CUT! THAT'S PERFECT!

The filming was over! And the kiss wasn't all that bad!
Sock Monkey and Lulu would both be stars.

WE'RE ALL DONE!
IT'S A WRAP!